Disney's PEPPER ANN
TOO COOL TO BE TWELVE.

Soccer Sensation

Created by
Sue Rose

Adaptation by
Nancy Krulik

Illustrated by
Stephanie Gladden

DISNEY
PRESS

New York

Story Editor
Nahnatchka Khan.
Based on a television script by
David Hemingson.

Copyright © 1998 by Disney Enterprises, Inc.

Printed in the United States of America.

First Edition

1 3 5 7 9 10 8 6 4 2

Library of Congress Catalog Card Number:98-72450

ISBN: 0-7868-4262-8 (paperback)

For more Disney Press fun, visit www.DisneyBooks.com

Soccer Sensation

CHAPTER ONE

Pepper Ann Pearson stared at the black and white ball. As the Hazelnut Otters' goalie, incoming soccer balls were a sight Pepper Ann had seen before.

"Okay, Weasels," Pepper Ann declared through gritted teeth. "Give me your best shot!"

Pepper Ann reached forward, jumped to meet the ball . . . and watched helplessly as it flew past her and into the goal cage.

"The score is four to zero," Trinket St. Blair, the soccer announcer, told the crowd. "Pearson can't seem to catch a ball, and the Otters can't seem to catch a break."

Trinket had just made the under-statement of the year. It was only the first game of the season, but already the Hazelnut Otters were starting their fourteenth consecutive losing season, the longest by far of any team in Hazelnut history.

Pepper Ann looked out over the field. Cissy Rooney, the Otters' center forward, had called a time-out to

reapply her Nuclear Reactor Red lip gloss.

The referee walked up to Cissy. "Ms. Rooney, sometime today?" he demanded.

But Cissy didn't answer. She just stared into space. Suddenly, Cissy collapsed in a heap! The crowd gasped. Coach Doogan raced to her side.

"Rooney. Rooney. Ya gotta speak to me," the coach cried out. Cissy blinked slowly, opened her eyes, and looked up at her coach's worried face.

"Uncle Frank? Is that you?" Cissy murmured in a daze.

Coach Doogan picked up Cissy's lip gloss. She dabbed a little on her finger and licked it carefully. "Here's the culprit," the coach declared.

"Looks like tainted lip gloss,"

Trinket shouted through her microphone.

As Cissy was carried off the field, Coach Doogan called for a time-out and gathered her players together.

"We need a replacement at center,"

she told the Otter girls. "Who's gonna sub for Rooney?"

No one volunteered. Center was the toughest position on the team. The center forward was expected to score the goals. So far, Cissy hadn't scored any goals, and even *that* seemed like a lot to live up to.

Pepper Ann looked down at a bucket of water. She saw her reflection on the side of the bucket.

"Hey, why don't you volunteer?" Pepper Ann's Alter Ego asked.

"But I'm the goalie," Pepper Ann replied.

Pepper Ann's Alter Ego frowned. "Face it. You *rot* at goalie. And besides, the *team* needs a center."

Pepper Ann took a deep breath, and looked away from the bucket. "Okay,"

Pepper Ann told Coach Doogan. "I'll do it for the team!" And with that, Pepper Ann raced out onto the field.

"Substituting at center is goalie Pepper Ann Pearson," Trinket announced.

Pepper Ann took her place in the center forward spot. The whistle blew. Dribbling the ball between her feet, Pepper Ann charged down the field. She moved to the right and to the left, avoiding Weasels with every turn.

Finally, Pepper Ann closed in on the Weasels' goal. She pulled back her leg and shot the ball toward the goal.

"SCORE!" Trinket shouted from the announcer's table.

Pepper Ann stared at the goal cage in disbelief. She had just scored the first Otter goal of the game! In fact, she'd scored the first Otter goal of the past eight years!

Pepper Ann's teammates ran over to congratulate her.

"Great shot," said Nicky Little, Pepper Ann's best friend and teammate since kindergarten.

"It was just luck," replied Pepper Ann modestly.

All through the second half, there was no stopping Pepper Ann. No matter where she was on the field, she managed to get her feet on the ball and score. When the final whistle blew, Trinket said the words the Otters had been waiting thirteen years to hear.

"We win! The Hazelnut Otters

defeat the Filbert Weasels in the most stunning upset in Middle School history!" Trinket declared.

The teammates hoisted Pepper Ann high onto their shoulders. The Otters' fans, all two of them, raced onto the field to join the celebration. Only Milo Kamalani, Pepper Ann's other best friend, was disappointed. Milo liked rooting for a record-breaking losing team. And up until now, the Otters were loser legends! Still, Milo couldn't help but be a little happy for Pepper Ann.

The next morning, as Pepper Ann got ready for school, she glanced into her mirror.

"Hey there, star!" her Alter Ego congratulated her.

Pepper Ann blushed red. Pepper Ann believed what Coach Doogan always said: A team working together is the whole enchilada. Individual players were just a bowl of chips without salsa. "Give me a break. I am not a star," Pepper Ann told her Alter Ego.

Pepper Ann's Alter Ego just laughed.

CHAPTER TWO

Pepper Ann walked slowly up the stairs to Hazelnut Middle School. It seemed like a normal day. A group of seventh-grade girls were busy staring at the impossibly cool eighth grader, Craig Bean. Craig was equally busy *not* staring back at them.

Then suddenly, someone spotted

Pepper Ann's mane of thick red hair . . . and everybody went crazy!

"Hey! It's Auburn Thunder!" one kid cried out. The kid held out his notebook to Pepper Ann. "You really rock! Can I have your autograph?"

That started it. Suddenly, kids were coming at Pepper Ann from all directions. They wanted autographs, pieces of her clothing, her shoes, even locks of her red hair!

"Whoa, Nelly!" Pepper Ann shouted. "Can I get a little room here?"

But the crowd wasn't about to move away. "Look! I got her scrunchy!" one kid shouted out as he held Pepper Ann's pony tail holder in his fist.

Pepper Ann ducked down low, crawled through a narrow hole in the sea of waving arms and legs, and ran

off. As soon as the kids realized that Pepper Ann had disappeared, they took off in search of her.

Pepper Ann's crazed fans chased her through the cafeteria, into the gym, behind the science labs, and into the girls' bathroom. Pepper Ann was finally able to ditch them behind a long row of lockers.

Pepper Ann's Alter Ego appeared reflected in a locker. "The star thing is pretty cool," it said slyly.

Pepper Ann shook her head. "Hey! I'm just a team player. And nothing, *nothing*, is going to change that!" she insisted.

"Hey, Pearson," Pepper Ann heard a familiar voice say. She got ready to run. But she stopped dead when she saw who was calling her. It was Craig Bean! Craig had barely even noticed Pepper Ann before—what with his being a cool eighth grader, and Pepper Ann being a lowly seventh grader.

"Nice moves," Craig told Pepper Ann. And then Craig did something miraculous. He lowered his sunglasses—if only for a second—to get a better look at Pepper Ann! Then he sauntered off.

Pepper Ann gulped. Craig Bean had spoken to her! She had to tell someone. Maybe Nicky. Or Milo. *Nah.* No one would believe her anyway.

Pepper Ann looked back at her Alter Ego and smiled. Maybe there was something to this star thing, after all.

CHAPTER THREE

At the next game, Coach Doogan put
Pepper Ann in at center again. This
time, Pepper Ann was all confidence.
She raced down the field, shaking off
the Lechee Nut Lemmings' defenders
with ease.

Pepper Ann became more daring and
showy—she   twirled   around   the

Lemmings' defense players, scoring every time.

Just after her sixteenth goal, Pepper Ann once again took control of the ball. Tessa and Vanessa, identical twins who wore the same number on their uniforms, moved into scoring position.

"We're . . . !" Tessa began.

"Open!" Vanessa continued, calling out to Pepper Ann.

But instead of kicking the ball to Tessa or Vanessa, Pepper Ann ran directly in between the twins, shot, and scored!

"Thanks to Pearson, the Otters win it, seventeen to zip!" Trinket announced to the crowd.

The Otter fans went wild. "Auburn Thunder! Auburn Thunder! Auburn Thunder!" they cried. Pepper Ann took a bow and flipped her hair back like a movie star.

But Pepper Ann's teammates were not as pleased with Pepper Ann's performance on the field as the kids in the stands were. The other Otter players turned away from Pepper Ann, and sulked back toward the locker room.

"Way to beat those Lemmings!" Coach

Doogan greeted the girls as they filed into the locker room. But the team did not look excited. They looked angry. "True, some of us had a better game than others. But that's okay! A goal for one player is a goal for us all," she added.

"Ah . . ." Tessa pointedly started.

"Hem," Vanessa even more pointedly finished.

The twins, like the rest of the team, weren't buying it.

"Of course, it is key to remember that no player is an island," the coach added. "Come on, what's the Otter motto?"

"Paws, claws, teeth, and fur. We're all part of *one* Ot-ter," all of the girls responded in unison—all of the girls except for Pepper Ann. She was too busy standing by the locker-room door signing autographs.

Coach Doogan watched Pepper Ann with concern in her eyes. Nicky Little was watching her, too. Nicky leaned over and whispered to the coach. "I'm sure it's just a phase," she assured her.

But Nicky wasn't so sure. She watched as Pepper Ann signed another autograph. Maybe this was just a phase. But by the looks of things it wasn't a phase Pepper Ann was going to give up any time soon.

CHAPTER FOUR

There was no way anyone at Halzelnut Middle School could have missed this year's biggest sports story—the rise of soccer superstar Pepper Ann Pearson—better known to her fans as Auburn Thunder.

In one short season, Pepper Ann had gone from lamest to famous, and from loser to cruiser. Pepper Ann put on a real show. She performed fancy footwork that was better than anything seen on a Broadway stage. The crowd loved her.

But while Pepper Ann was gaining the affection of the crowd, she was losing the respect of her teammates. And that fact wasn't lost on Trinket.

"One question weighs on everyone's mind," Trinket announced to the sellout crowd at the Otters' final game before the championship. "Is she still the same down-to-earth team player that she used to be? Or has success spoiled Pepper Ann?"

Success had definitely spoiled Pepper Ann. And as her friend, Nicky knew she had to help her. But bringing

Pepper Ann down to earth was too big a job for Nicky to take on alone. She needed Milo's help. So Pepper Ann's two best friends (her two *only* friends) decided to set her straight.

Milo and Nicky spent Saturday afternoon looking for Pepper Ann. They finally tracked her down holding court at Brain Dead, the local arcade hangout.

"Why are we here?" Milo complained

to Nicky. "It's been weeks since that 'winner' gave us the time of day."

"Because things are getting worse. And as her best friends, we need to say something," Nicky insisted.

Nicky and Milo walked past rows of video games and grabbed Pepper Ann by her arms. They carried her behind the arcade and plopped her on top of a garbage Dumpster.

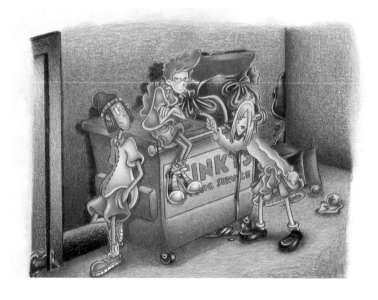

Nicky reached up and removed Pepper Ann's dark sunglasses from her face. She wanted to look Pepper Ann in the eye. Pepper Ann opened her mouth to protest, but Nicky stopped her.

"Don't talk, just listen," Nicky ordered. "You've changed, Pepper Ann. Your soccer success has made you distant and aloof. And worst of all, you've forgotten your teammates."

Pepper Ann looked at Nicky and smiled. "No, I haven't, Mickey," she replied.

"It's Nicky," her friend told her sternly.

"Whatever," Pepper Ann said, tossing her auburn hair over her shoulders.

"Listen. You should thank me," Pepper Ann continued. "If I hadn't stepped in to center, we'd still be losers. Now we're playing in the championship."

Nicky shook her head slowly. "The other kids were right," she told Pepper Ann. "The glory has gone to your head. You've turned into . . . one big otter butt!" And with that, Nicky grabbed Milo and pulled him away from the Dumpster.

"The glory has *not* gone to my head!" Pepper Ann shouted after them.

Pepper Ann sat there, alone at the top . . . of a heap of smelly garbage. As she turned to climb down from the Dumpster, Pepper Ann glanced in the store window.

"AAAHH!" Pepper Ann shouted in fear. She couldn't believe what she saw. It was Pepper Ann's Alter Ego. But

it looked like a huge, red-headed
monster.

"Look at me!" the Alter Ego shouted
angrily at Pepper Ann. "I'm hideous.
You've got to chill out, or I'm gonna
explode!"

Pepper Ann didn't want to hear it. She hopped off the Dumpster and laughed defensively. "I'm a star," she told her Alter Ego as she walked away. "If you don't like it, wear a hat!"

CHAPTER FIVE

On the day of the championship game, the team suited up in their Otter uniforms. They took their places on the locker-room benches and waited for Coach Doogan's pep talk.

"Now get out there and win, win, win!" the coach shouted, finishing her speech. The girls ran out onto the field.

As Pepper Ann stood up and

prepared to saunter onto the field, Coach Doogan pulled her aside.

"Not you, Pearson. You're benched."

Pepper Ann was so surprised, she took off her sunglasses. "BENCHED?!" she shouted. "I can't be benched!"

"Why not?" Coach Doogan asked her. "You never show up for practice; you're surly; you're selfish; and you're late, late, late! It looks like *somebody* has forgotten that there's no 'I' in team!"

Pepper Ann was angry. After what she had done all season for this sorry team, the coach was pulling her now? "But there's a 'me' in team," Pepper Ann sputtered defensively.

Coach Doogan wasn't going to accept that. "Sorry, Pepper *Anagram*. I'm going with a real team player."

Just then, Nicky ran back into the locker room. Pepper Ann gasped. Nicky was wearing Pepper Ann's number!

"Nicky?" Pepper Ann asked in disbelief. "But she's never even laced up her cleats!"

"Don't you worry, missy," Coach Doogan replied. "We'll be just fine."

But the Otters were *not* fine without Pepper Ann. In fact, by halftime they were losing big-time.

"It's a real bloodbath out there. Without Pearson, these Otters are easy prey for the title-hungry Pinenut Possums," Trinket declared. "Ooo, I just grossed myself out," she added with a shiver.

Pepper Ann sat on the bench and glanced at a bucket of water. Her Alter Ego stared back at her. The head was so big, it couldn't fit in the bucket.

"What're you doing?" the Alter Ego asked Pepper Ann.

"This is me waiting for an apology," Pepper Ann responded.

Pepper Ann's Alter Ego laughed. "Hello? Wake up and smell the arrogance. Coach Doogan's the one who deserves an apology."

Pepper Ann looked away. "Why don't you just leave me alone?" she muttered.

"Okay," the Alter Ego agreed. "But remember this. You can't escape the truth. Every time you primp in the mirror, I'll be there. Every time you sign a glossy photo, I'll be there. Every time you watch a highlight reel, I'll . . . be . . . THEEERE!"

Pepper Ann looked at her Alter Ego. The head was getting larger and larger. It was bubbling and sputtering.

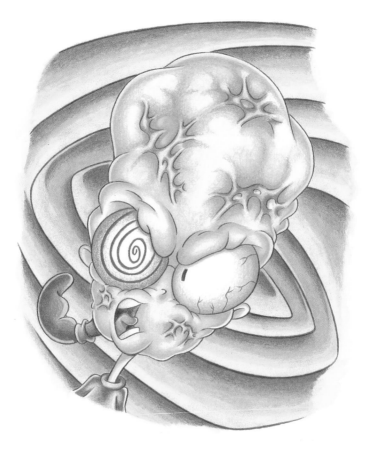

Pepper Ann had created a big-headed, egomaniacal monster! And that monster was herself!

There was only one thing she could do. Pepper Ann apologized to Coach Doogan for acting like a jerk.

Coach Doogan smiled warmly. "Apology accepted," she said.

"I just wish there was some way I could make it up to the team," Pepper Ann said.

"You can get out there and save our bacon!" Coach Doogan told her.

But Pepper Ann shook her head. "I can't rob Nicky of her moment in the sun," she said.

Just then Pepper Ann heard a hollow *thud* followed by a loud moan. She looked over at the field. A Possum player had just collided with Nicky, and Nicky lay in a crumpled, groaning mess on the ground.

Pepper Ann raced out onto the field. She didn't wave to the crowd or show off in any way. Instead, she helped her friend over to the bench to rest.

"Wait! Pearson's taking the field!" Trinket called out excitedly.

Pepper Ann tried to ignore the dirty looks she received from her own teammates as she took her place at center.

"The other Otters look a little peeved, but this Pearson seems different. She's . . . changed," Trinket told the crowd.

Pepper Ann really had changed. Instead of keeping the ball all to herself, Pepper Ann gladly passed it to her teammates. The Otters were a team again. And as a team, they managed to score goal after goal, while keeping the Possums from scoring anything!

"This game is more exciting than my fall wardrobe!" Trinket excitedly told the crowd. "Pepper Ann has brought the team back from certain death to tie with the Possums, nine to nine!"

At just that moment, Pepper Ann stole the ball from the Possums' center player. As she kicked the ball down the field, Pepper Ann looked up toward the clock. There were only seconds left to play!

Pepper Ann raced toward the goal. She noticed Tessa and Vanessa. The twins were completely open. But Pepper Ann herself was in the perfect position to make the winning goal. What should she do?

Pepper Ann gritted her teeth and made her final kick.

CHAPTER SIX

The ball soared down the field, across the Possums' goal cage, and toward Tessa and Vanessa. Vanessa cocked her foot and kicked, sending her shoe flying into the air while the soccer ball sat motionless at her feet.

Tooot! The final whistle blew. The

game was over. Pepper Ann looked up at the scoreboard. *"We tied!"* she shouted out excitedly.

Trinket spoke for many of the fans as she said, "So ends the greatest season of Otter soccer ever. Not with a bang, but with an *eh*." Trinket looked at her lilac-blue, perfectly manicured nails. "Sure, some of us are disappointed, but we must remember one thing. By

announcing games instead of playing, I've fulfilled my entire PE requirement without breaking a single nail!"

So Trinket was happy, and the team was happy. But it was Pepper Ann who was the happiest of all. She'd discovered that she was a phenomenal soccer player. But more importantly,

Pepper Ann had learned to become a team player.

"Paws, claws, teeth, and fur. We're all part of one Ot-ter!" Pepper Ann led the team in their cheer as they headed back into the locker room.

And this time, Pepper Ann really meant it.